W9-AAQ-690

Author's Note

I first visited Skara Brae in the summer of 1978. The Orkney Islands, north of Scotland, and all their marvelous archaeological sites fired my imagination. I became fascinated with what life must have been like in prehistoric times. I have returned four times to the Orkneys to sketch, paint, and photograph their many ancient monuments.

This book is based on fact. I have, however, made some assumptions concerning certain aspects of the prehistoric village of Skara Brae. For example, it is not known exactly how the roofing of the huts was constructed. I followed the theory that the village inhabitants used whalebone, slates, and heather sods on top of corbeled walls. Also, burial mounds associated specifically with Skara Brae are not known. But, burial mounds in the Orkneys such as Maes Howe, Unstan Cairn, and others are more or less contemporary with the village, and similar mounds could have been built by the inhabitants of Skara Brae. There are unexcavated burial mounds in the immediate vicinity of the village. I used Maes Howe as the model for the cairn shown in this book.

I have tried to tell the story of the village in a lively and artistic manner by adding hypothetical details without straying too far from the facts.

I hope the story of Skara Brae will encourage people to visit the Orkney Islands in all their splendor, and to see for themselves the village of the hilly dunes.

written and illustrated by

Olivier Dunrea

Holiday House / New York

SKARA BRAE

The Story of A Prehistoric Village

For RICHARD L. SMITH, a great teacher and dear friend, who will live always in my heart.

I would like to thank Margery Cuyler, David Rogers, John and Kate Briggs, and Barbara Walsh for their unflagging faith and trust in me throughout this project.

I am grateful to Bernard Wailes, Associate Professor of Anthropology at The University Museum, The University of Pennsylvania, for reading the manuscript and offering his professional comments and encouragement on the book. Also, I owe thanks to the Philadelphia branch of the English-Speaking Union, especially to Margaret Arnott, James Bryson, and Nancy Hoyle, for awarding me the Cooper/Woods Award travel grant in 1981 which helped me tremendously in my research for this book.

I give special thanks to Susan Evans, Dugalda Wolfson, and Eric Johnson for the use of their photographs, taken at Skara Brae during an expedition sponsored by the Academy of Natural Sciences of Philadelphia. I extend a very warm thanks to David Nicholson of Kirkwall, Orkney Islands, who sent me much needed current material concerning Skara Brae and its excavation reports.

Finally, my greatest thanks and gratitude go to Edward Boyer for his unending moral and artistic support in getting this book finished.

Library of Congress Cataloging in Publication Data

Dunrea, Olivier.
Skara Brae: the story of a prehistoric village.

SUMMARY: Describes the Stone age settlement preserved almost intact in the sand dunes of one of the Orkney Islands, how it came to be discovered in the mid-nineteenth century, and what it reveals about the life and culture of this prehistoric community.
1. Skara Brae Site (Scot.)—Juvenile literature.
2. Neolithic period—Scotland—Juvenile literature.
3. Excavations (Archaeology)—Scotland—Juvenile literature.   4. Orkney—Antiquities—Juvenile literature.   5. Scotland—Antiquities—Juvenile literature.   [1. Skara Brae Site (Scot.)   2. Man, Prehistoric.   3. Stone Age.   4. Archaeology]
I. Title.
GN776.22.G7D85   1986   936.1′132   85-42882
ISBN 0-8234-0583-4

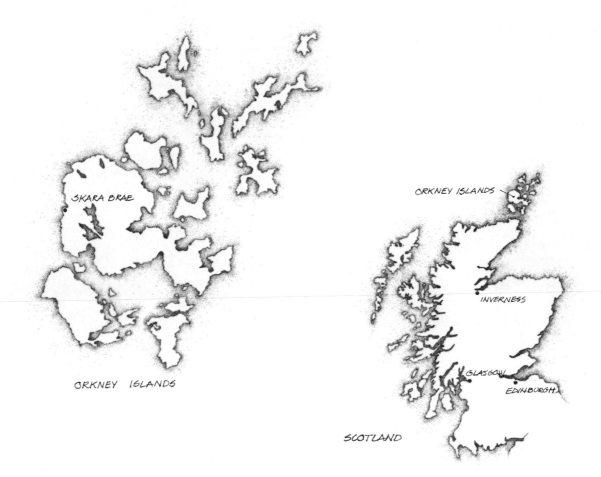

SKARA BRAE

ORKNEY ISLANDS

ORKNEY ISLANDS

INVERNESS

GLASGOW

EDINBURGH

SCOTLAND

By the year 6000 B.C.—eight thousand years ago—a great migration had begun. Slowly people from the Near East were moving westward into Europe.

It was still the Stone Age. Later, in the Neolithic ("New Stone") Age, people had settled in Europe and were practicing farming and herding. But as Neolithic man needed more space and more food, he began to move again.

By 3500 B.C. farmers and herders had reached a group of islands to the north of Scotland—the Orkneys.

They found the Orkneys an ideal place to live. There were gently rolling hills, open grassland for their sheep and cattle, and wide, sand-fringed bays. The islands had no predatory animals that would attack their livestock. It was a good area to settle.

Orkney was a strange place to these early settlers. They were accustomed to trees and forests. In Orkney there were far fewer trees.

But though there was very little wood, there was plenty of fuel. Mosses and other plants had decayed in bogs to form peat. The peat could be burned like coal. The settlers could keep warm and cook their meat around a peat fire.

Most of all, there was a great abundance of stone on the islands. Stones were everywhere—on the beaches, on the grasslands, and on the hills. The Neolithic herders and farmers chose these stones to build their permanent homes and monuments.

In time the Orkneys became more populated. New masses of migrating people reached their shores. Several generations of settlers came and went, and some ventured off to the smaller and lesser populated islands.

One band of settlers, seeking better grazing land for their animals, moved farther out on the main island. Making their way to the farthest west coast, they explored the land for a suitable place to live.

As they marched northward along the rugged cliffs and inlets, they came to a beautiful wide bay—the Bay of Skaill. There were sand dunes, open grassland, and no other settlers to compete for the land's resources. It was here the band decided to make their new home.

There were twenty people in the group: four small families. Together they owned a flock of sheep, a small herd of cattle, and a few pigs.

After surveying the land around the bay, they chose the
southwest corner in which to erect their temporary shelters. The
women and older children put up the tents, using wooden poles
they had brought with them. These tents made of skins would
protect them from rain and wind.

It was the task of the older children to tend the livestock, even
though the animals mostly fended for themselves and found food
wherever they could.

During this period, settlers lived off their animals. To their
diet of meat and milk they added wild foods foraged from the
land and sea—birds and eggs, fish, shellfish such as limpets, and
wild grains. The men sometimes brought in the meat of deer and
other wild animals as well.

Through the summer, autumn, and winter the band continued
to live in their tents. During the winter months they started construction of a new village that would have proper houses for all
the families.

While they built the permanent stone houses, everyone worked. The men gathered the larger stones needed for the foundations and walls. The women and children also gathered stones to be used in the construction of the huts.

Everyone worked together on all the houses. One partly completed house was used as a shelter for the cattle, sheep, and pigs. The band continued to live off their animals as well as the land and sea.

There were plenty of stones on the beach around the bay, and collecting them went quickly. The stones could be easily split to make straight, uniform surfaces for building.

The stones were laid one on top of another without the use of mortar. We now call this method of building drywall construction.

The settlers might have used curved whalebones washed up on the beach to help support the roofs.

The houses were small when completed, measuring only twelve feet long by six to nine feet wide in the interior.

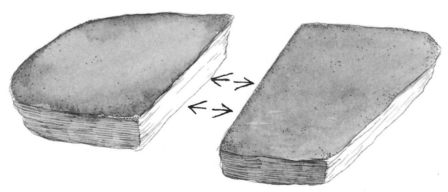

FRESHLY SPLIT
SURFACES WERE STRAIGHT

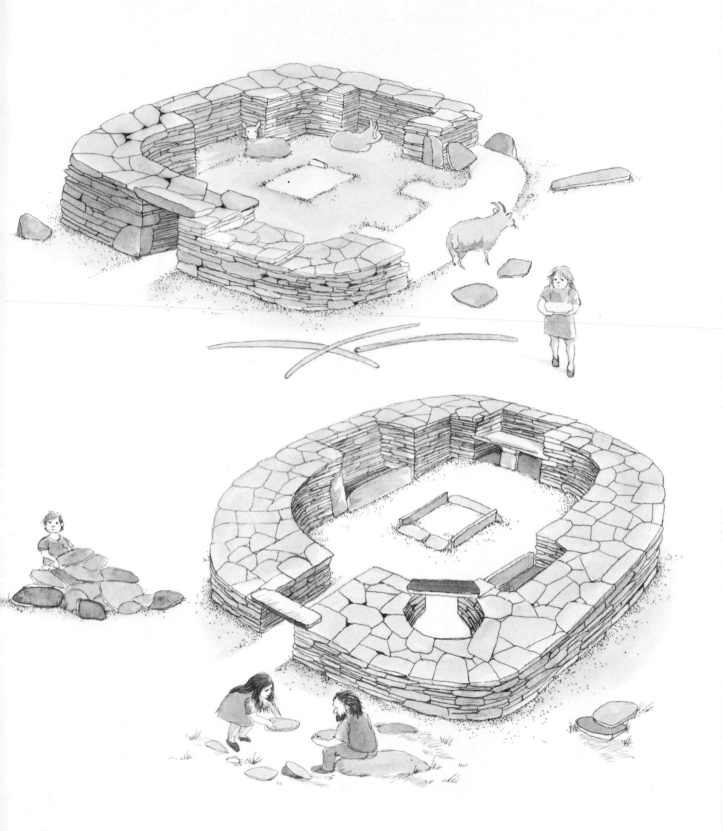

The plan of each house was basically square, with rounded corners.

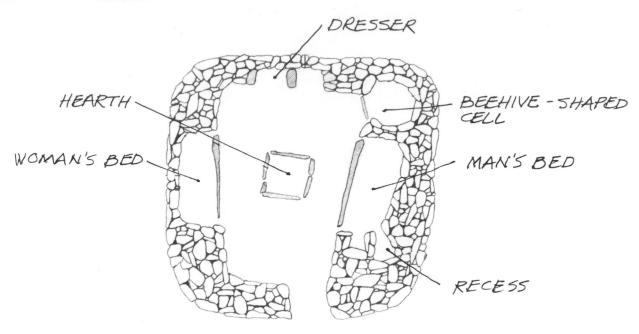

In one of the corners, there was a small, beehive-shaped cell, used either for storage or as a latrine.

The walls were built by piling stone upon stone. A few feet above the floor the stones began to project a little toward the inside of the hut. This overlapping construction is called corbelling.

Each hut was big enough to allow room for a central hearth, a stone bed set into the wall on either side of the hearth, and a stone dresser built into the rear wall. The mother and small children slept in the bed to the left of the hearth; the father slept in the bed to the right.

The stone beds were filled with heather and skins, making them comfortable and warm for sleeping.

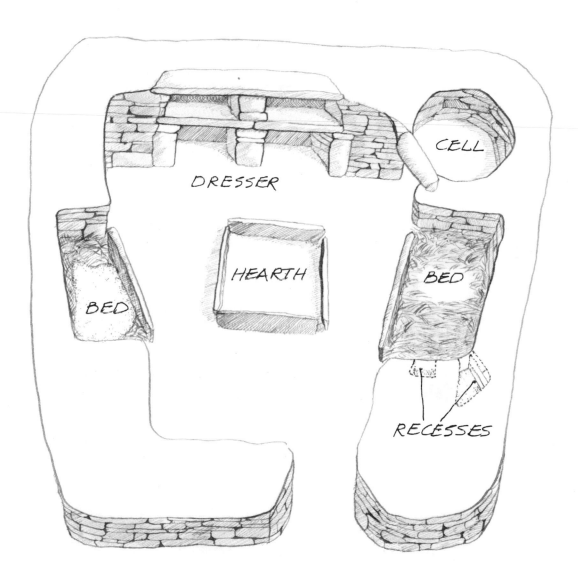

There were one or two small recesses for keeping personal possessions in the wall above each bed.

Within a few weeks the little huts were completed. And so began the occupation of the village. It was around 3100 B.C.

As they went about the routine of their daily life, the villagers allowed their refuse to pile up against the outside walls of their huts. Shells, broken bones, fragments of pottery, sand, and everything no longer used was heaped around the structures.

This refuse, called midden, helped to insulate the huts. It kept
the cold winds from blowing through the chinks in the stones.
Over the years these midden heaps mixed with sand and became
a claylike covering from which grass grew.

Now the huts looked like the surrounding dunes of the Bay of
Skaill. And thus came into existence the village we now call
Skara Brae—the village of the hilly dunes.

As the generations came and went, so did the huts. The older huts were sometimes taken down stone by stone to build new huts.

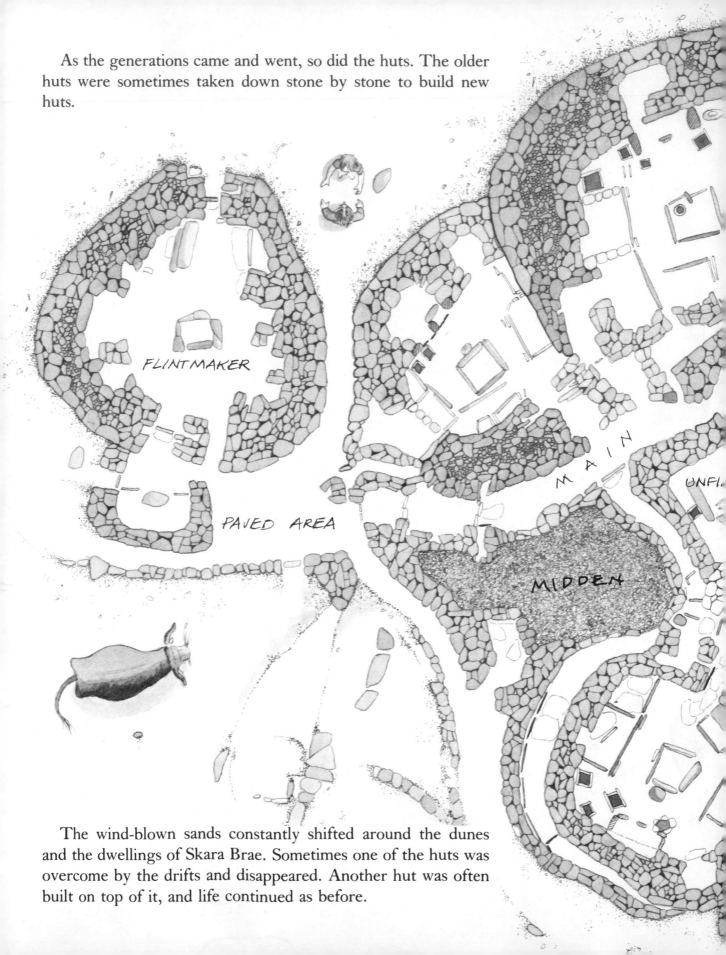

FLINTMAKER

PAVED AREA

MAIN

UNFI...

MIDDEN

The wind-blown sands constantly shifted around the dunes and the dwellings of Skara Brae. Sometimes one of the huts was overcome by the drifts and disappeared. Another hut was often built on top of it, and life continued as before.

MEN BUILDING A HOUSE

WOMEN MAKING POTTERY

PASSAGE

MIDDEN AND STONE INFILLING

PAVED AREA

STONE BASIN

HOUSE

EARLIER ABANDONED HOUSES

The shifting sands and the ever-increasing midden heaps continually changed the appearance of the village. Other changes also took place. The newer huts were built to be larger and more comfortable.

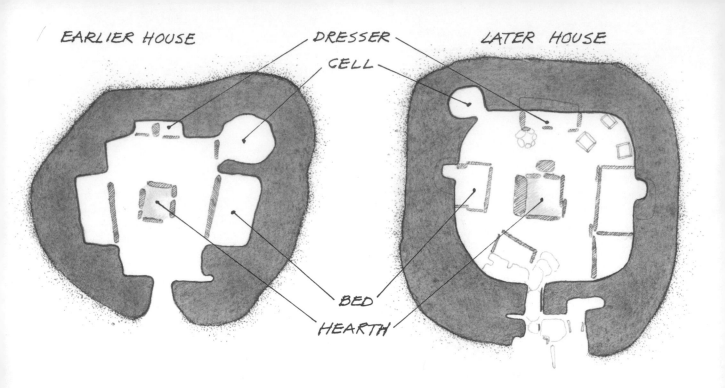

The beds had stone pillars at each corner supporting a canopy made of skins. The stone dresser was now built against the rear wall and was no longer set into it.

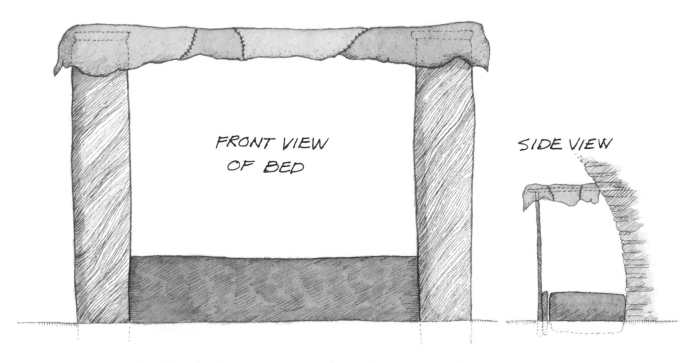

Inside, the hearth remained the focal point of the room. The stone beds, however, were no longer built into the walls but projected out into the room. Sometimes a third bed was added for the children.

The collecting of limpets, a kind of shellfish, had become increasingly important to the villagers. Limpet shells were heaped in great quantities around the huts along with the other refuse.

In the floor of the huts the villagers built stone boxes carefully sealed with clay to make them watertight. In these holding tanks they kept their limpets in the water for later use as bait or perhaps as food. Several tanks were built so that there could always be a ready supply of limpets.

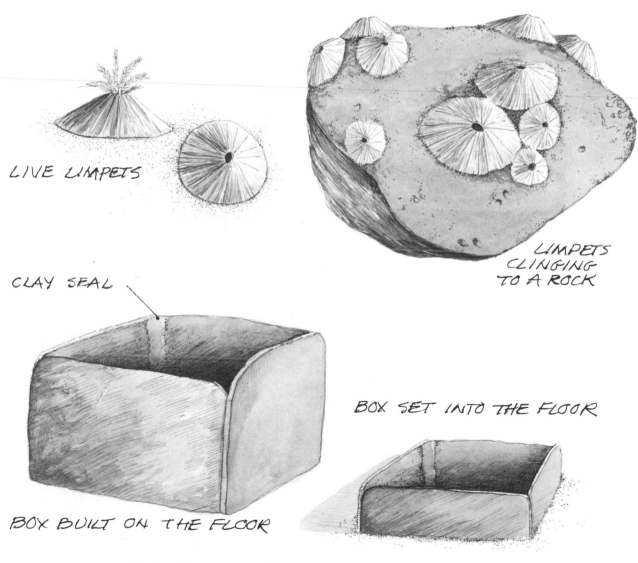

LIVE LIMPETS

LIMPETS CLINGING TO A ROCK

CLAY SEAL

BOX SET INTO THE FLOOR

BOX BUILT ON THE FLOOR

STONE LIMPET BOXES

At some point in their history the inhabitants of Skara Brae most likely began to cultivate small plots of grain. They remained an isolated group, living a quiet life off the land and sea and their stock of animals.

As the village grew, so did its population. The villagers were bound together by common need, common activity, and the beliefs and ceremonies that characterized all Stone Age peoples.

Evidence of one of these beliefs was found underneath a wall of one of the later huts. Two aged women of the village had died. Their bodies were buried beneath the wall in the hope and belief that their spirits would support the wall and help sustain the life of the village. This was the only time the villagers performed this rite. Henceforth the dead would be buried in communal burial mounds.

When the settlers were first building their permanent homes, there was little time for anything else. Several generations later, the village was well established and had settled into an ordered pattern of life. The villagers now attended to other matters. They were able to focus on the social and ceremonial life that keeps a community together.

For the Neolithic villagers of Skara Brae, one such shared activity might have been the construction of a communal burial mound, or cairn.

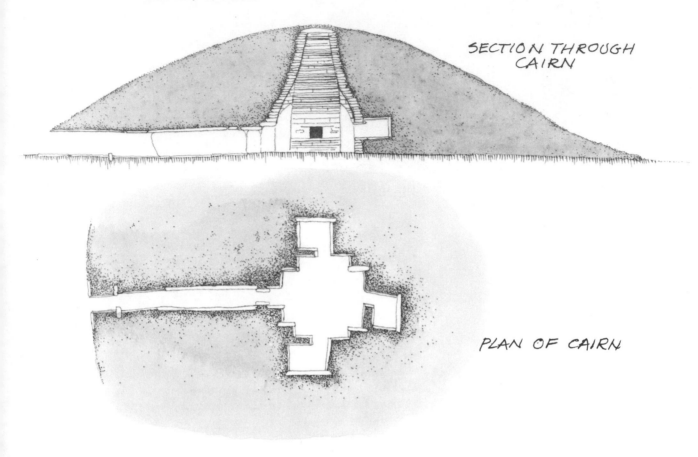

SECTION THROUGH CAIRN

PLAN OF CAIRN

The construction of the cairn took longer than that of the huts because it was much larger. Once it was completed, it served generation after generation.

The exterior of the cairn was covered with earth, and in time grass grew over it. It looked like a hill in the landscape.

ENTRANCE TO CAIRN

There was also time for the villagers to practice their various crafts. The women made pottery. Sometimes they made engraved or raised designs on their pots. But the people of Skara Brae, unlike many Neolithic peoples, were not especially skilled at this craft.

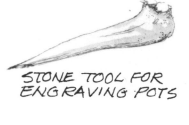

STONE TOOL FOR ENGRAVING POTS

TYPICAL CLAY POTS

CARVED STONE BALL

BONE TOOLS FOR PIERCING

TOOL FOR CARVING

The men spent hours carving strange, intricate patterns on stone balls.

The teeth and bones from sheep, cattle, and whales were used to make beautiful beads and necklaces.

TEETH CARVED INTO BEADS

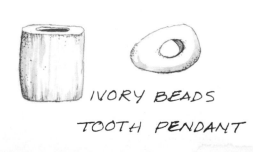

IVORY BEADS

TOOTH PENDANT

TOOTH BEADS

For a long time the life of Skara Brae continued uninterrupted. Then, around 2400 B.C., when the village had settled into its way of life, a terrible catastrophe occurred that caused it to be abandoned forever.

As the villagers went about their daily tasks of collecting food and tending their herds or practicing their crafts, a sudden and violent storm arose. The storm came so unexpectedly and with such severity that the inhabitants fled without being able to collect all their belongings.

In her haste to escape, one woman broke her string of beads as she squeezed through the narrow doorway of her hut. The necklace fell to the floor of the passageway, and there it remained.

In another hut an old man was gnawing a choice bit of mutton when the storm took him by surprise. He dropped the bone by his bed and fled the hut in panic.

Then the wind-driven sands quickly filled all the stone huts, burying the necklace and the half-eaten bone for the ages.

The storm raged with a fury the villagers had never experienced before. They fled the village in blind terror.

The sea pounded in the bay, and to the prehistoric people of Skara Brae it must have seemed that the world was coming to an end.

The villagers abandoned their village in the hilly dunes. Several times a small number of them returned and camped under the remaining exposed walls of the huts. And then they never returned again. Over the centuries the sand continued to drift in, until nothing was visible.

Although the name Skara Brae remained, memory of the village itself vanished.

It was not until over 4,000 years later, in the winter of 1850, that another severe storm befell the Bay of Skaill and changed its appearance once more. The storm stripped the grass and sand from the dunes and exposed to view the stone walls and midden heaps of Skara Brae's huts. Observers were astonished.

The Laird of Skaill, William Watt, who owned the land, began to explore this remarkable site. Throughout Orkney there were many prehistoric burial mounds and other monuments for archaeologists to examine, but this was the first settlement ever discovered.

By 1868 four of the huts had been cleared, and a good number of relics and artifacts had been found. Then Skara Brae was once again seemingly forgotten by man.

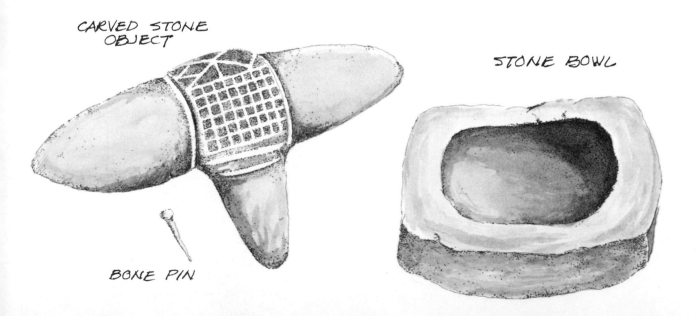

CARVED STONE OBJECT

STONE BOWL

BONE PIN

In December 1924 Skara Brae experienced yet another violent storm. The storm washed away part of the midden covering one of the huts and damaged portions of the previously cleared dwellings.

The Commissioners of His Majesty's Works took action. They had a strong seawall built to protect the huts from further damage. At the same time, the Commissioners asked V. Gordon Childe, an archaeologist, to excavate the village of Skara Brae.

From 1927 to 1930 the site was uncovered, and six new dwellings were brought into view.

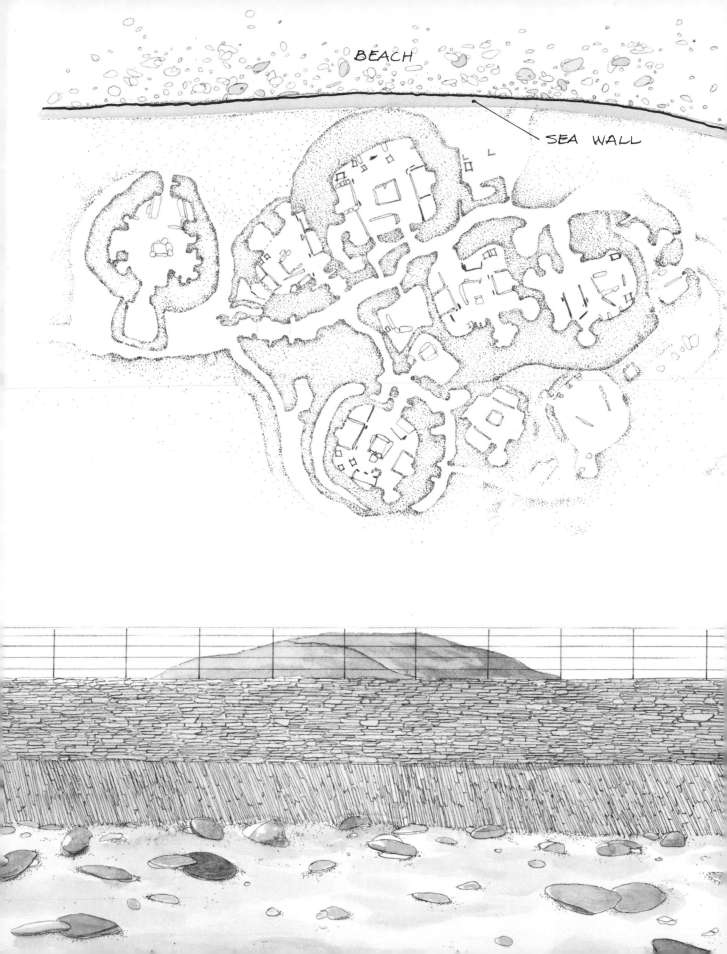

BEACH

SEA WALL

It was difficult for the archaeologists to believe this village could actually be the work of prehistoric peoples. The huts were neatly and efficiently designed, even by twentieth-century standards.

There was a paved area that could have been a marketplace and a separate structure that probably was a flint-worker's shop.

V. Gordon Childe and his team carefully cleared out all the sand from the huts.

The sand had perfectly preserved everything. The archaeologists recorded their findings and drew plans of the huts and their arrangement.

Everything was built of stone!

During the excavation the archaeologists hired a local woman to cook for them. She moved into one of the prehistoric huts and lived there quite comfortably throughout the project.

The Neolithic people had built their village and monuments with expertise. Thus it was odd to find only the crudest and most rudimentary pieces of pottery.

POTTERY   FRAGMENTS

STONE BALL

IVORY PIN

There were, however, some beautifully and strangely carved stone balls.

The artifacts, pottery, and other relics were carefully cleaned and sent off to a museum.

The archaeologists were especially impressed with a beautiful broken string of beads lying on the floor of one of the passageways.

BONE-PIERCING TOOL

PIN MADE FROM WALRUS IVORY

BEAD NECKLACE

TOOTH PENDANT

Through careful uncovering and painstaking documentation of the placement of all the furnishings and relics, the archaeologists were able to piece together the story of this remote village on the Bay of Skaill in the Orkney Islands.

In 1972 another archaeologist, D. V. Clarke, reexamined the site. Clarke's team came upon objects that gave them new clues about life at Skara Brae—charred bits of grain, fish bones, and pieces of rope that had been woven from strands of heather. Using more modern tests to date these finds, Clarke discovered that Skara Brae was even older than Childe had thought.

FRAGMENT OF ROPE

MEASURING STICK

MEASURING TAPE

For over 4,000 years the stone village of Skara Brae had been lost to mankind.

Now, more than 5,000 years after its first construction and occupation, people can once more visit the islands north of Scotland and see the stone huts and stone furnishings of Skara Brae—the village of the hilly dunes.